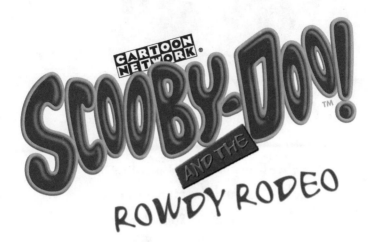

CARTOON NETWORK

SCOOBY-DOO!

AND THE

ROWDY RODEO

D0109017

Look for the **Scooby-Doo Mysteries**.
Collect them all!

ROWDY RODEO

Written by
James Gelsey

A
LITTLE APPLE
PAPERBACK

SCHOLASTIC INC.

New York Toronto London Auckland Sydney
Mexico City New Delhi Hong Kong Buenos Aires

For Brittany and Samantha

ISBN 0-439-28484-8

Designed by Carisa Swenson

12 11 10 9 8   3 4 5 6/0

Special thanks to Duendes del Sur for cover and interior illustrations.
Printed in the U.S.A.
First Scholastic printing, November 2001

Chapter 1

The Mystery Machine cruised down the highway. Fred was driving, with Daphne and Velma next to him in the front seat. Shaggy and Scooby were in the back, studying a road map.

"No, Scooby, you've got it upside down," Shaggy said. "The lake is up there and the mountains are over there."

"Ruh-uh," protested Scooby. "Rook." He pointed toward the windshield with his paw. Some mountains were visible straight ahead. He looked back at the map.

"I give up!" Shaggy announced. "Like, why won't you tell Scoob and me where we're going?"

"Because we don't want to hear you two complaining for the whole trip about whether there's going to be any food there," Daphne replied. "Besides, using the map to try to figure it out has kept the two of you very busy."

"And very quiet," added Velma.

"Hey, we don't always complain about food," Shaggy protested. "Do we, Scoob?"

Scooby thought for a moment and then nodded his head.

"Rup!" he barked.

"If you really want to know where we're going, I'll give you a hint," Daphne offered. "It has to do with yodeling."

"Rodeling?" asked Scooby. "Rhat's rhat?"

"It's a singing sound that goes back and forth from low to high," Velma explained.

"Shaggy, why don't you show Scooby how a yodel sounds?" asked Fred.

"I don't know how to yodel," Shaggy replied.

"Sure you do," Daphne said. "And I'll prove it. Knock, knock."

"Who's there?" asked Shaggy.

"Little old lady," Daphne said.

"Like, little old lady who?" asked Shaggy.

Fred, Velma, and Daphne started laughing. "There. You did it, Shaggy. You just yodeled!"

"I did?" Shaggy said with surprise.

"Say that line again," Daphne coached. "Only this time, make your voice go high and low."

"Little old lady who," Shaggy sang, changing his voice along the way.

"That's a yodel, Scooby," Daphne said.

"Rike ris?" asked Scooby. He cleared his throat with a loud cough. He threw back his head and let out a howl. "Rodel-rady-rodel-rady-rodel-rady-hee-rooooooo!"

"Boy, that was terrific, Scooby!" Fred smiled. "Bucky will be amazed!"

"Excuse me, but who's Bucky and what does yodeling have to do with where we're going?" interrupted Shaggy.

"All right, we'll tell you," Daphne relented. "We're going to the Bucky McCoy Rodeo."

"In the old days, Bucky McCoy was a famous movie star," Velma continued. "He was called 'The Yodeling Cowboy.'"

"I used to watch his movies all the time when I was a kid," Fred added. "I was even president of his fan club."

Shaggy and Scooby looked back at the map.

"I can't find Bucky McCoy's anything on the map," Shaggy said. "We really must be in the middle of nowhere."

"Ranches usually are, Shaggy," Velma explained.

"I guess it doesn't matter," Shaggy said. "As long as there's —"

"Don't worry, Shaggy, there'll be plenty of food," Fred answered. He steered the Mystery Machine into a dusty parking area and found a spot.

"In that case," Shaggy called, "let's giddyap!"

Chapter 2

The gang piled out of the van and walked toward the front of the wooden rodeo stadium. The words BUCKY MCCOY'S RODEO were spelled with horseshoe-shaped letters over the entrance. People dressed in all kinds of cowboy clothes were going inside.

Just outside the entrance, a small crowd of people gathered. Some were holding up pictures and cowboy hats and cameras. As the gang got closer, they noticed two people standing in the middle of the crowd. They were smiling, waving, and signing autographs.

"That must be Bucky McCoy!" Fred said.

"And who's that with him?" asked Daphne.

"That's Pokey Jones, his sidekick," Fred explained. "Every cowboy star had a side-kick."

Fred led the others over to the crowd. He caught Bucky McCoy's eye and waved.

"Hi, Mr. McCoy," Fred called. "It's me, Fred Jones!"

Bucky squinted at Fred. Then a big smile appeared on his face. He raised a finger and called back, "Just a minute!"

He turned to the crowd and said a few words. The people slowly walked away and into the stadium. Then Bucky and Pokey joined Fred and the gang.

Bucky was dressed like a real cowboy. He wore a blue shirt, dark blue dungarees, black-and-white chaps, dusty brown cowboy boots, a red bandanna around his neck, and a tall white ten-gallon hat.

"How-dy, Freddie!" Bucky exclaimed. "You're a sight for sore eyes." Bucky grabbed Fred's hand and gave his whole arm a shake.

"You remember Freddie Jones, don't cha, Pokey?" Bucky asked his sidekick. "He was the best president the Bucky McCoy Fan Club ever had!"

Pokey wore a plaid shirt, a black vest, and baggy dungarees. "How do?" he said, tipping the undersized cowboy hat resting on his head.

"These are my friends, Daphne, Velma, Shaggy, and Scooby-Doo," Fred said, introducing everyone.

"Welcome, y'all," Bucky said. "This your first time at a rodeo?"

"Yes, sir," Daphne answered.

"Aww, forget those formalities with me, young lady," Bucky said. "All my friends call me Bucky."

"And yer enemies call ya a no-good, lyin', cheatin' varmint," a nearby voice yelled. A tall, skinny man with a long white beard and dusty old overalls stomped over. "Jist what is this?" the man asked, waving a long, skinny piece of paper at Bucky.

"You know what that is, Zane," Bucky answered. "It's the rodeo show card. It lists all the cowboys in the order they're going to appear."

"I know what it is! Jist what's the big idea of having a rodeo without telling me?" Zane yelled back. "And another thing. When were ya gonna tell me about that fence? Or weren't ya?"

"What fence, Zane?" asked Bucky.

"You know darn tootin' what fence!" Zane yelled back. "The one that's two feet on my property, over by the stream. Now you get that thing moved proper or you're gonna hear from my grandson the lawyer. And when he's done with you, you'll be wearin' a lawsuit instead of that moth-eaten cowboy suit!"

The man turned and stormed away.

"Who was that?" asked Fred.

"Just an ornery little critter," Pokey said.

"That's Zane Hatfield," Bucky said. "He's my neighbor. Our families have been feuding for years. It's been so long, in fact, that none of us can remember how the whole thing

even started. All I know is that he's been looking for every excuse he can think of to get me
off this land. The thing is, he may get his
wish."

"How come?" asked Daphne.

"Nobody's interested in old cowboys any-
more." Bucky sighed. "I can barely afford to
keep this ranch going. That's why I'm holding
this rodeo. I need to raise some money. I've
got a few other ideas, but none of 'em will
matter if this rodeo doesn't work. Anyways,
I'd better go check out that fence . . . just in

case. Pokey, do me a favor and show the kids inside."

Bucky slowly walked off after Zane.

"Like, excuse me, Mr. Pokey, but is there a snack bar around?" asked Shaggy. "Scoob and I would love a little pre-rodeo snack."

"No snack bar," Pokey said. "But there's the chuck wagon out back."

"What's a chuck wagon?" Shaggy whispered to Scooby.

"Ri runno," Scooby answered.

"Well, whatever it is, I hope you can eat it," Shaggy replied.

Chapter 3

The gang followed Pokey Jones around the outside of the rodeo stadium. They passed a row of horse trailers attached to pickup trucks. Some cowboys were hanging around, talking. One of them was playing with a long brown rope. He looped it up into his hands, made a couple of twists, and then started spinning it up in the air. Very quickly, a lasso started circling above their heads.

"Wow! What a groovy trick," Daphne said.

The cowboy spinning the lasso nodded at

Daphne and tipped his hat. As he did, he lost his concentration and the lasso fell right on top of him.

"You kids wanna see a real lasso? I'll show you a real lasso!" a loud man hollered as he ambled over to the gang. His cowboy outfit looked more like a costume than real clothes.

"Jinkies, is he a real cowboy?" whispered Velma.

"By the looks of it, I'd say he's a coupla cowboys rolled into one," Pokey answered.

The man came over and started spinning a lasso in the air. He kept the lasso spinning as he jumped up and down, moved the rope

14

from hand to hand, and even held it in his mouth.

"Wow, that's pretty impressive," Fred commented.

"Ya think so?" asked Pokey. "Watch this."

Pokey reached up and stopped the spinning rope. Instead of falling down into a pile of limp rope, the lasso kept its shape and plopped down onto the ground.

"Hey, that's not a real lasso," Daphne exclaimed.

"You're right, Daphne," Fred said. "That's one of those trick lassos. It looks like a rope, but it's really a plastic loop that keeps its shape no matter what."

The big cowboy blushed a little.

"The chuck wagon's just around back, that way," Pokey said. "I'll go on ahead and see what they've got ready."

"Sorry about that, folks," the large cowboy said. "Just having a little fun. The name's

Moulash. Alvin Moulash. But my cowboy friends call me 'Slim.'"

"Are you here to see the rodeo, too, Mr. Moulash — I mean, Slim?" asked Daphne.

Alvin "Slim" Moulash looked around and then leaned in toward the gang.

"Truth be told, I'm not really a cowboy," he confessed. "I'm a real estate agent. And I've been sizing up the property because I heard that Mr. McCoy isn't doing too well financially, if you know what I mean. And I'm just bursting to show somebody what I found. But you've got to promise not to tell anyone."

Slim Moulash reached into his pocket and took out a long piece of paper.

"Hey, what's this?" he said, looking at it. "Oh, it's the show card. I was looking for that." Slim Moulash stuffed the card into his vest pocket and reached further into the other pocket. He pulled out a red bandanna that looked like it was holding something. He

put the bandanna on the palm of his right hand and opened it up with his left. Five little golden pebbles shimmered in the sunlight.

"Gold!" Shaggy exclaimed.

"Shhhhhhhhhhhhh!" Slim said, quickly closing his hand. He looked around to see if anyone had heard Shaggy. Then he slowly opened his hand again. "I found these in a stream at the far corner of the property. And they're going to make me a very rich man. Once I buy the property from Bucky McCoy, that is. Of course, I'm counting on you to keep this our little secret. And as a token of my appreciation, I'll be happy to set a few of these little nuggets aside just for you."

"Are you still here, Alvin?" Bucky called as he walked over to the group. "I thought you left a while ago."

"I did, but I decided to come back to see the rodeo," replied the real estate agent. Alvin secretly stuffed the nuggets back into his pocket. "And to see if you've given some more thought to my offer."

"Thanks, but no thanks," Bucky said. "Something really terrible would have to happen before I ever sold the ranch."

"We'll see about that," muttered Slim as he stalked away.

Chapter 4

Bucky and the gang continued around back and found the chuck wagon. It was a real covered wagon set up like a cowboy snack bar. Trays of all kinds of delicious-looking foods lined the counter.

"Man, that sure looks good," Shaggy said.

"Rou raid it!" Scooby agreed, licking his lips.

"This is really set up just for the cowboys in the rodeo, but help yourself, pardners," Bucky said.

"Like, thanks, Bucky!" Shaggy exclaimed.

"Come on, Scooby! Let's get some grub."

They walked over to the counter of food.

"Like, I don't know where to start, Scoob," Shaggy gasped.

"How about at the end of the line?" a deep voice said from behind.

Shaggy and Scooby turned and saw a tall, stocky cowboy holding an empty plate.

"Sorry about that," Shaggy gulped. He and Scooby stood aside as the big cowboy made a huge barbecue sandwich.

"Bronck Paddock!" Bucky called as he walked over. "These kids are my guests, and as long as you're at my rodeo, I expect you to show them a little courtesy."

"You see, Bucky, this is what I've been

trying to tell you," Bronck replied. "You're never gonna keep this ranch and this rodeo going if you keep bringing in this kind of crowd. I've got two words for you, Bucky," Bronck continued. "Extreme rodeo. Or as I like to call it, 'X-rodeo.' Trust me, Bucky, you'll be rolling in dough before you know it."

"Unlike you, Bronck, I will never turn my back on my cowboy heritage to make a quick buck," Bucky said. "All you want to do is strip away the majesty and mystery of the whole cowboy experience."

"All I want to do is make the rodeo exciting and fun!" Bronck snapped back. "Face it, Bucky, you're the cowboy of the past. And I'm the cowboy of the future."

Bronck stared back at Bucky. He ate his barbecue sandwich in two enormous bites. Then, as Pokey walked by with a plate of his own, the cowboy reached out and grabbed the red bandanna hanging out of Pokey's back pocket. He wiped his mouth with it and stuffed it into his own pocket.

"Thanks for the grub, Bucky," Bronck said and walked away.

"Extreme rodeo?" asked Fred. "What's that?"

"Bronck's idea is to take regular rodeo and cowboy things and make them more dangerous," Bucky tried to explain. "Like instead of roping a calf, a cowboy would try to rope a snapping crocodile. Blindfolded."

"That doesn't sound very safe to me," Daphne commented.

"Speaking of safe, is it safe to eat now?" Shaggy asked.

"You bet, Shaggy!" Bucky said. "But make it quick, 'cause we're going to be starting the rodeo real soon. I have to go saddle up Betsy. I'll see you kids later."

Bucky walked over toward the stables behind the chuck wagon.

"Come on, Scoob," Shaggy said. "Let's eat!"

Chapter 5

A little while later, the gang made their way into the stands to watch the rodeo. One cowboy roped three different calves with a single lasso. Another cowboy did some riding tricks on the back of his horse. And another rode a bucking bronco for one full minute, one arm gripping the reins and the other flailing around in the air with each mighty kick of the horse. When the minute was up, a bell rang and a clown jumped up out of a barrel that was standing off to the side of the ring.

"Hey, what's that clown doing?" asked Shaggy. "I thought this was a rodeo, not a circus."

"That's a rodeo clown," Fred explained. "They help out. Just watch."

The cowboy jumped off the bucking horse and ran over to the fence. The clown ran right in front of the horse and then started running in the opposite direction. The horse chased the clown around the ring, allowing the cowboy to get out safely. The crowd laughed as the clown did some silly leaps and somersaults. A couple of horse handlers came into the ring and led the horse away.

The clown tipped his hat to the crowd and ran out, too.

"See, Shaggy? That's what rodeo clowns do," Daphne said.

Music started playing over the loud-speakers.

"Ladies and gentlemen, please welcome the star of the silver screen, Bucky McCoy, the Yodeling Cowboy, and his sidekick, Pokey Jones!" announced a voice.

Everyone cheered as Pokey walked out into the ring. He was leading an old but beautiful chestnut-brown horse. Bucky McCoy sat atop the horse, holding his guitar. He smiled and waved to the crowd.

"It's Betsy!" Fred exclaimed. "That's Bucky's horse from the movies."

Pokey walked the horse once around the ring and then into the middle. Bucky grabbed his guitar and started singing one of his most popular songs, "The Yodeling Day." It was a series of yodels put to music. When he finished, the crowd jumped to its feet and roared with applause.

"Hey, there's another one of those clowns!" Shaggy said.

A rodeo clown had stood up inside one of the barrels in the ring. Bucky looked over and then gave a questioning look to Pokey. Pokey shrugged. The clown had so much trouble climbing out of the barrel that it tipped over. Everyone laughed at the silly clown.

Then the clown ran over to one of the gates along the rear of the ring. He climbed up on top of it and shouted to the crowd.

"Ladies and gentlemen!" he yelled. "It's time to hit the trails! This rodeo is officially and forever-ly closed!"

The clown jumped down and opened the gate. An angry bull charged into the ring, heading right for Bucky and Betsy. Pokey ran and jumped into one of the barrels. Betsy was barely able to outrun the bull, but she managed to get out of the ring safely.

Then the clown opened the other two gates, releasing a couple of bucking broncos

into the ring. The bull charged the stands, ramming the fence with his horns. The crowd screamed and people started running for the exits.

"Hey, where'd the clown go?" asked Daphne.

"I don't know, and I don't care," Shaggy replied. "Like, let's get out of here!"

"Oh, no you don't," Velma said. "We're not going anywhere."

"Velma's right," Fred said. "It looks to me like we've got a mystery to solve."

The gang watched the bull and two broncos run through one of the open gates and out the back of the ring.

"As long as we have the chance, let's start looking down in the ring," Fred said.

The gang made their way down to the ring and hopped over the fence. Bucky came through one of the open gates and looked around. Pokey stuck his head out from the barrel.

"Coast clear?" he asked.

"I can't believe this," Bucky sighed. "My rodeo is ruined. And so are my chances to keep the ranch."

"Don't worry, Bucky," Fred said. "You take care of rounding up the horses and that bull, and we'll take care of rounding up the clues to solve this mystery."

"And I think I've already lassoed one," Velma called. She stood next to the tipped-over barrel, peering inside. She reached in and came out with a long piece of paper.

"It's a rodeo show card," she said.

"See, Bucky?" Fred asked. "We're on our way."

"Good luck, kids," Bucky said. "Come on, Pokey. We've got a lot of roundin' up to do."

"And we've got a lot of detective work to do," Daphne added.

Chapter 6

"We'd better split up," Fred said. "Daphne and I will look for more clues around the rodeo ring."

"If that rodeo clown is still around, he may be hiding," Velma stated. "Shaggy, Scooby, and I will see what we can find."

"Sounds good," Fred agreed. "Let's meet back by the chuck wagon as soon as we can."

"Speaking of the chuck wagon," Shaggy said. "How about we drop by now for a quick bite? Scooby and I hate looking for clues on an empty stomach."

"Forget it, you two," Velma said. "No more snacks until we solve this mystery. Now let's get to work."

Shaggy and Scooby followed Velma across the rodeo ring and through one of the open gates. They walked through a narrow stall and out an open gate on the other side. A large barn stood in the distance. The chuck wagon was off to the right. Immediately in front of them stood bales of hay, some large bags of horse feed, some ropes, horse blankets, saddles, and some other cowboy equipment.

"I'll start on this side, and you two look over there," Velma instructed as she disappeared behind a pile of hay.

"Okay, but don't blame us if we faint from hunger," Shaggy warned. "Come on, Scoob."

Shaggy and Scooby looked at the piles of horse equipment lying all over the ground.

"Like, I don't even know what kind of

clues we're supposed to be looking for, do you, Scooby?" Shaggy asked.

"Ruh-uh," Scooby replied, shaking his head. "Romething rownish?"

"I suppose something clownish." Shaggy nodded. "But what about something foodish first?"

"Rokay!" barked Scooby.

They walked over to the chuck wagon and found it closed.

"Just our luck, Scoob," Shaggy complained. "Maybe there's a back door. Come on."

Shaggy led Scooby around to the back of the chuck wagon. Shaggy tried the back door, but it was locked, too.

"Nope, this one's locked, too, Scoob," Shaggy said. "Scoob? Scooby-Doo, where are you?"

"Rover here!" Scooby called. His voice sounded muffled. Shaggy looked around and didn't see Scooby anywhere. Then he heard a soft munching sound coming from a tall metal cabinet next to the door. Shaggy opened the door and peered inside.

"Ri, Raggy!" barked Scooby. He had barbecue sauce all over his whiskers and held the remains of a sandwich in his paws.

"Scooby! Shaggy! What are you doing inside that food cabinet?" Velma scolded. "I thought I told you this was no time for snacking."

"Rorry, Relma," Scooby apologized.

"Now come out of there, Scooby," Velma said. "And wipe your mouth. You've got barbecue sauce all over your face."

Scooby licked all the sauce off with his big tongue.

"Here, Scoob, use this," Shaggy said, handing Scooby a red bandanna.

"Shaggy, where'd you get that bandanna?" asked Velma.

"Right over there," Shaggy said, pointing to small box on the ground next to the cabinet. Velma picked up the box and looked inside.

"Jinkies!" she exclaimed.

"What is it?" asked Shaggy.

"It's a makeup kit," Velma said.

"Come on, Velma, you don't need any makeup," Shaggy said. "You're beautiful just as you are."

"Not that kind of makeup," Velma explained. "It's clown makeup. And along with that red bandanna, I'd say we found another clue."

"Just think, Velma, if Scoob and I hadn't come over to get something to eat, we'd never have found the clue," Shaggy said.

"That's not all you'd never have found," a strange voice called from around the side of the chuck wagon. Suddenly, the rodeo clown jumped out and roared at the three friends.

"Zoinks! Let's get out of here!" Shaggy yelled.

Chapter 7

The rodeo clown chased Velma, Shaggy, and Scooby around the chuck wagon three times. Then Velma jumped behind some of the hay bales while Shaggy and Scooby ran toward the big barn with the rodeo clown right behind them.

As Velma peered out from behind the hay, Fred and Daphne ran over from the rodeo ring.

"Is everything all right?" Daphne asked.

"The rodeo clown is after Shaggy and Scooby!" Velma exclaimed.

Fred, Daphne, and Velma ran down the

dirt path toward the barn and saw Shaggy and Scooby disappear inside. The clown stopped at the door and looked off to his left.

"Hmm, that's interesting," Velma said.

The three of them watched as Betsy slowly walked over to the barn. The clown reached out his hand and gently grabbed her reins. He led the horse over to a hitching post next to the barn and then looked up at the top of the barn. The hitching post was right beneath an opening in the hayloft.

"What's he doing?" Daphne wondered.

The clown looped the reins over the hitching post, then ran into the barn.

"It looks like he's after Shaggy and Scooby again," Fred said. "Come on."

Inside the barn, Shaggy and Scooby were hiding under a horse blanket in one of the stalls.

"Quit hogging all the blanket, Scooby," Shaggy complained. "That clown's going to find us for sure if you keep pulling the blanket off me."

"Rorry, Raggy," Scooby apologized.

"Shhhhh!" Shaggy said. "Listen. I think I hear big clown footsteps."

The sounds of feet shuffling through the hay got louder and louder.

"Oh, no!" Shaggy whispered. "He's going to get us! What'll we do?"

Suddenly, the blanket flew up into the air. Shaggy and Scooby clutched each other and closed their eyes tight.

"All right, you two, you can come out now," Daphne said. Shaggy opened one eye and saw Daphne, Fred, and Velma standing in front of them. Fred and Velma were holding the blanket.

"Whew!" Shaggy sighed. "For a minute there, we thought you were that creepy clown."

"Speaking of the clown, did you happen to see where he went?" Fred asked.

"Like, we were too busy inspecting this blanket for clues," Shaggy said.

They heard a scratching sound and saw some hay flutter down to the ground. Everyone looked up at the wooden boards on the ceiling. Small wisps of hay were falling through the cracks.

"I think we've found our clown," Velma said. The gang tiptoed over to the ladder leading up to the hayloft. Just as Fred poked his head up into the hayloft, he saw the clown standing by the opening.

"We've got you now!" Fred warned. He and the others started toward the clown, who smiled at them, turned, and jumped.

"Zoinks! The clown jumped out the window!" Shaggy exclaimed.

The gang ran over to the opening and looked down. They saw the clown lying in a pile of hay beneath the window. He got up and ran back toward the chuck wagon and rodeo ring. Betsy was eating from a bale of hay, her reins dragging on the ground.

"So that's why he tied up Betsy," Fred said. "He planned to jump on her from up here and make a quick getaway. After scaring Shaggy and Scooby, of course."

"It looks like Betsy had other plans," Daphne said.

"Jinkies! That's it!" Velma exclaimed. "I have a hunch that this rodeo clown is headed for his last roundup."

"Velma's right," Fred said. "Gang, it's time to set a trap."

Chapter 8

"The only way we're going to get that clown to come out again is to make him believe that the rodeo's still going on," Fred said.

"But all the horses have run away," Shaggy pointed out.

"Not all of them, Shaggy," Daphne answered, pointing to Betsy.

"But all the cowboys are gone," Shaggy added. "Like, what kind of rodeo can you have without cowboys?"

"A Scooby-Doo and Shaggy kind of rodeo," Daphne said, smiling.

"Oh, no," moaned Shaggy. "Not us. No way."

"Ruh-uh," Scooby echoed. "Ro ray."

"But we really need your help, Scooby," Daphne pleaded. "Would you help out for another visit to the chuck wagon later?"

Scooby thought a moment and then shook his head.

"Then how about a visit to the chuck wagon later and a Scooby Snack now?" offered Velma.

Scooby's eyes lit up. His tail started wagging furiously.

"Rokay!" he barked.

Daphne tossed a Scooby Snack.

Scooby kept his eye on the snack  and then grabbed it — lassolike — with his tongue. He chomped it down and let out a small burp.

"Rorry," he apologized, grabbing his stomach. "Roo ruch rarbecue."

"Now listen up, because we don't have much time," Fred said. "Scooby, Daphne will dress you up like Bucky. Shaggy, you're going to pretend to be Pokey, so you can walk Betsy around the ring. Velma will go to the announcer's booth and put on one of Bucky's records to make it look like Scooby's singing. Meanwhile, I'll be hiding in one of the barrels with a lasso. When the clown shows up, get him to chase you over to my barrel. I'll jump up and rope him. Everyone got that?"

The rest of the gang nodded.

"Then let's get into position," Fred said.

Daphne took Shaggy and Scooby over to the area behind the rodeo ring. She found enough bits and pieces of different cowboy outfits to put together one for Scooby and

one for Shaggy. She even found Bucky's guitar resting against a bale of hay.

Fred walked Betsy over to the ring. Then he grabbed a rope and hid in one of the barrels.

Velma made her way up to the announcer's booth. Soon everyone was ready.

"Okay, good luck, fellas," Daphne said. "I'm going to get the real Bucky and let him know what's happening."

Shaggy wore baggy dungarees, a dusty vest, and a tan cowboy hat that was two sizes too large. Scooby sat high in Betsy's saddle. He wore a tall tan ten-gallon hat, a black-and-white cowskin vest, and a pair of furry chaps over his rear legs. Bucky's guitar was between his paws.

"Riddyap!" he barked.

Shaggy picked up the reins and slowly walked Betsy into the rodeo ring. When Velma saw them enter the ring, she started the recording. Music began playing through the loudspeakers.

"Get ready, Scoob, I mean, Bucky," Shaggy whispered. "Here's your cue."

Scooby grabbed the guitar and pretended to play and sing one of Bucky's yodeling songs. Just then, the clown ran through one of the open gates and into the ring.

"Let's go, Betsy!" Shaggy yelled. He jerked her reins and started leading the horse toward Fred's barrel, hoping the clown would follow. Betsy, however, decided she didn't want to move.

As the clown got closer to them, he reached into his costume and pulled out a whip. The clown snapped it into the air twice.

"Zoinks!" Shaggy exclaimed.

Upon hearing Shaggy's voice, Betsy suddenly lurched into action. She raised up on her rear legs and let out a loud whinny. Then she started charging around the ring. Scooby

held on with all his might as Betsy ran after the clown and Shaggy.

"Now, Fred!" Shaggy yelled as they neared the barrel. Fred jumped up and tossed out his lasso. Just as he did, Shaggy's hat fell over his eyes, causing him to trip and knock into the clown. The clown fell to the ground and the lasso landed around Shaggy.

The clown scrambled back to his feet and saw Betsy close behind him. Betsy suddenly stopped running and kicked her back feet up into the air. Scooby couldn't hold on any longer. He went sailing through the air and landed with an enormous *PLOP* right on top of the clown!

Chapter 9

Bucky and Pokey ran into the ring just as Scooby went flying through the air. Bucky let out a short whistle, and Betsy suddenly stopped kicking. Bucky grabbed her reins and stroked her long nose.

"Good job, girl," he said.

"And good job to you kids," Pokey added. "Looks like you done wrangled yourselves a clown."

"Bucky, would you like to see who was behind all this?" asked Fred.

"You betcha," Bucky answered, handing

Betsy's reins to Pokey. Bucky walked over and helped Scooby up. Then he raised the clown to his feet. Bucky took a bandanna out of his own pocket and wiped the makeup off the clown's face.

"Alvin Moulash!" Bucky exclaimed.

"Just as we suspected," Velma said.

"You did?" asked Pokey. "How in tarnation did you know?"

"Well, it wasn't easy at first because we had three suspects," Daphne explained. "Zane Hatfield, Bronck Paddock, and Mr.

Moulash here all had reasons for wanting to ruin the rodeo and get Bucky to sell the ranch."

"And the first clue we found confirmed that any of them could have been the clown," Fred said. "It was the rodeo show card Velma found in the barrel. The clown needed it to see when Bucky was coming out. And all three of the suspects would have needed one."

"But then we found the second clue, which eliminated Zane," Velma stated.

"Eliminated me from what?" Zane asked angrily as he walked into the ring. "Did you leave me out of something again, McCoy?"

"Shaggy and Scooby found a red bandanna with some clown makeup on it," Velma continued. "And we remembered that Mr. Moulash had a red bandanna as part of his cowboy costume."

"And Bronck Paddock took mine and got it all barbecue-sauced up," Pokey added.

"Exactly," Fred confirmed.

"Which made the last clue so important," Daphne said. "And the last clue wasn't something we found but something we observed. We saw the clown tie Betsy to the hitching post under the barn. He planned to jump from the hayloft and onto Betsy's back."

"Like you used to do in the movies, Bucky," Pokey interjected.

"But when the clown jumped, we saw that Betsy had walked away," Fred said. "That means that the clown didn't tie the reins properly, like a real cowboy would have."

"And Bronck Paddock, whatever his faults, is a real cowboy," Pokey agreed. "He'd never let something like that happen to him."

"So why'dja do it, Moulash?" asked Bucky.

Alvin Moulash fidgeted a bit and then let out a deep breath. He reached into his pocket and took out a handful of the gold pebbles.

"I found these in a stream on the edge of your property," he explained. "I wanted to ruin the rodeo so you'd have no choice but to sell the ranch. I was going to get you to sell it to me, and then I was going to mine the gold and become rich, rich, rich."

A smile started spreading across Bucky's face and grew into a full-fledged yodeling laugh.

"What's so funny?" demanded Alvin.

"You are," Bucky replied. "That's not real gold. Those are pebbles covered with gold paint. I put them out there as an experiment."

"That stream flows onto my property, too," Zane complained. "What kind of experiment were you doing with water flowing onto my land?"

"I put those gold stones there to see if the paint would last," Bucky explained, "as part of my idea to create a little gold mining town for kids. You know, turn part of the ranch into a little Old West theme park for families. They could come and pan for gold, see a show in the saloon, and then come to the rodeo."

"What a great idea, Bucky!" Daphne exclaimed.

Just then, Betsy walked over behind Scooby and gave him a nudge.

"Ruh?" he said.

"Betsy feels bad about that last ride she

gave you," Bucky said. "She wants to give you a real ride now."

Pokey helped Scooby into Betsy's saddle. As Betsy trotted around the ring, Scooby grabbed his hat and waved it in the air.

"He sure looks like a real cowboy," Bucky said.

"You mean cowdog!" Shaggy joked. Everyone laughed.

"Scooby-Dooodle-layhee-doodle-layhee-doodle-layhee-Dooo!" called Scooby.

About the Author

As a boy, James Gelsey used to run home from school to watch the Scooby-Doo cartoons on television (only after finishing his homework). Today, he still enjoys watching them with his wife and two daughters. He also has a real dog named Scooby who loves nothing more than a good Scooby Snack!